MICHAEL DAHL PRESENTS

SUPER FUNNY
JOKE BOOKS

KNOCK
YOUR
SOCKS
OFF

A BOOK OF
KNOCK-KNOCK
JOKES

PICTURE WINDOW BOOKS
a capstone imprint

MICHAEL DAHL PRESENTS SUPER FUNNY JOKE BOOKS

are published by Picture Window Books
a Capstone Imprint
151 Good Counsel Drive, P.O. Box 669
Mankato, Minnesota 56002
www.capstonepub.com

Who's There?, *Ding Dong, Door Knockers, Nutty Neighbors*, and *Open Up and Laugh*
were previously published by Picture Window Books, copyright © 2004

Library of Congress Cataloging-in-Publication data
is available on the Library of Congress website.
ISBN: 978-1-4048-5774-2 (library binding)
ISBN: 978-1-4048-6371-2 (paperback)

Art Director: KAY FRASER
Designer: EMILY HARRIS
Production Specialist: JANE KLENK

PHOTO CREDITS

Shutterstock: bicubic (p. 47), Dietmar Höpfl (p. 44), djdarkflower (p. 37), FreeSoul
Production (p. 7, 22), Iznogood (p. 42), Joseph (p. 14), Kheng Guan Toh (p. 26, 62),
Michael Monahan (p. 30), Miguel Angel Salinas Salinas (p. 13), pichayasri (p. 46),
Robert Forrest (p. 39), sonia.eps (p. 42), venimo (p. 66).

KNOCK, KNOCK.

WHO'S THERE?

DWAYNE.

DWAYNE WHO?

DWAYNE THE BATHTUB, IT'S OVERFLOWING!

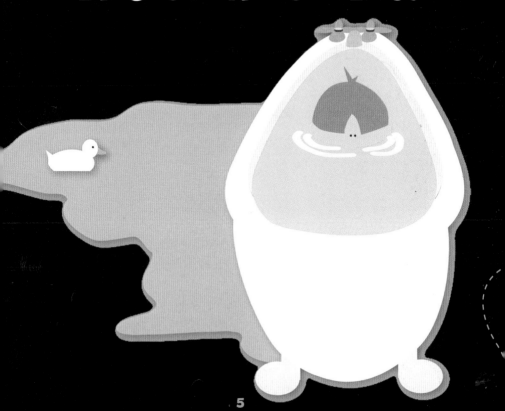

Knock, knock.

Who's there?

Ivan.

Ivan who?

Ivan out here for hours, and you still won't open the door!

Knock, knock.

Who's there?

Gorilla.

Gorilla who?

Gorilla my dreams, I love you!

Knock, knock.

Who's there?

Ice cream.

Ice cream who?

I scream, you scream,
we all scream for ice cream!

Knock, knock.

Who's there?

Henrietta.

Henrietta who?

Henrietta whole cake!

Knock, knock.

Who's there?

Champ.

Champ who?

Champoo your dog.
He's got fleas.

Knock, knock.

Who's there?

Freeze.

Freeze who?

Freeze a jolly good fellow.

KNOCK, KNOCK.

WHO'S THERE?

DORIS.

DORIS WHO?

DORIS LOCKED, THAT'S WHY I'M KNOCKING!

Knock, knock.
Who's there?
Amos.
Amos who?
A mosquito bit me.

Knock, knock.
Who's there?
Annie.
Annie who?
Annie bit me again!

Knock, knock.

Who's there?

Elsie.

Elsie who?

Elsie you later.

Knock, knock.

Who's there?

Little old lady.

Little old lady who?

I didn't know you could yodel!

Knock, knock.

Who's there?

Catsup.

Catsup who?

Catsup in the tree!

Knock, knock.

Who's there?

Harry.

Harry who?

Harry up and answer the door!

Knock, knock.

Who's there?

Abby.

Abby who?

Abby stung me on the nose.

Knock, knock.

Who's there?

Tennis.

Tennis who?

Tennis five plus five.

Knock, knock.

Who's there?

Butter.

Butter who?

Butter not tell,
it's a secret!

Knock, knock.

Who's there?

Yule.

Yule who?

Yule never know unless you
open the door.

KNOCK, KNOCK.

WHO'S THERE?

COWS GO.

COWS GO WHO?

NO, COWS GO "MOO."

Knock, knock.

Who's there?

Hutch.

Hutch who?

Please cover your mouth when you sneeze.

Knock, knock.

Who's there?

Anita.

Anita who?

Anita tissue.

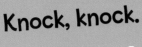

Knock, knock.

Who's there?

Peeka.

Peeka who?

Peeka boo, of course.

Knock, knock.

Who's there?

Four eggs.

Four eggs who?

Four eggsample.

Knock, knock.

Who's there?

Cash.

Cash who?

I didn't realize you were a nut!

Knock, knock.

Who's there?

Eskimo.

Eskimo who?

Eskimo questions, and I'll tell you no lies.

Knock, knock.

Who's there?

Weasel.

Weasel who?

Weasel while you work!

Knock, knock.

Who's there?

Heaven.

Heaven who?

Heaven you heard enough knock-knock jokes?

Knock, knock.

Who's there?

Hi.

Hi who?

Hi ho! Hi ho! It's off to work we go!

Knock, knock.

Who's there?

Tori.

Tori who?

Tori I bumped into you.

Knock, knock.

Who's there?

Megan.

Megan who?

Megan a cake. Do you have any eggs?

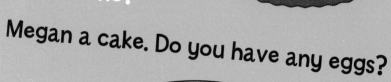

Knock, knock.

Who's there?

Juicy.

Juicy who?

Juicy who threw that
snowball at me?

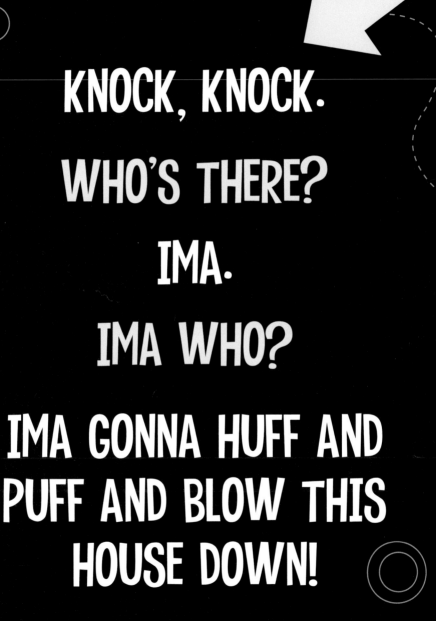

KNOCK, KNOCK.

WHO'S THERE?

IMA.

IMA WHO?

IMA GONNA HUFF AND PUFF AND BLOW THIS HOUSE DOWN!

KNOCK, KNOCK.
WHO'S THERE?
DAKOTA.
DAKOTA WHO?

DAKOTA'S TOO BIG FOR ME. MAY I BORROW YOURS?

Knock, knock.

Who's there?

Turnip.

Turnip who?

Turnip the heat, it's cold in here.

Knock, knock.

Who's there?

Handsome.

Handsome who?

Handsome of those cookies to me.

Knock, knock.

Who's there?

Ben.

Ben who?

Ben knocking so long my hand hurts!

Knock, knock.

Who's there?

House.

House who?

House it going?

Knock, knock.

Who's there?

Water.

Water who?

Water you doing at my house?

Knock, knock.

Who's there?

Wooden shoe.

Wooden shoe who?

Wooden shoe like to know?

Knock, knock.

Who's there?

Adam.

Adam who?

Adam up, and tell me the score.

Knock, knock.

Who's there?

Statue.

Statue who?

Statue making all that noise?

Knock, knock.

Who's there?

Queen.

Queen who?

Queen as a whistle!

Knock, knock.

Who's there?

Ivan.

Ivan who?

Ivan my money back.

Knock, knock.

Who's there?

Alpaca.

Alpaca who?

Alpaca the lunch for the picnic.

Knock, knock.

Who's there?

Ketchup.

Ketchup who?

Ketchup with me, and I'll tell you.

Knock, knock.

Who's there?

Radio.

Radio who?

Radio not, here I come.

Knock, knock.

Who's there?

Wah.

Wah who?

Well, you don't have to get so excited about it!

Knock, knock.

Who's there?

Dozen.

Dozen who?

Dozen anybody ever
answer the door?

Knock, knock.

Who's there?

Tish.

Tish who?

Why yes, I'd love a tissue.

33

KNOCK, KNOCK.

WHO'S THERE?

DEWEY.

DEWEY WHO?

DEWEY HAVE TO KEEP
LISTENING TO THESE
KNOCK-KNOCK JOKES?

Knock, knock.

Who's there?

Luke.

Luke who?

Luke out!

Knock, knock.

Who's there?

Clair.

Clair who?

Clair the way, I'm coming through!

Knock, knock.

Who's there?

Avenue.

Avenue who?

Avenue heard me knocking all this time?

Knock, knock.

Who's there?

Roach.

Roach who?

Roach you a letter, but you never wrote back.

Knock, knock.

Who's there?

Pasture.

Pasture who?

Pasture bedtime, isn't it?

Knock, knock.

Who's there?

Tuba.

Tuba who?

Tuba toothpaste.

Knock, knock.

Who's there?

Justin.

Justin who?

Justin time for dinner.

Knock, knock.

Who's there?

Darrel.

Darrel who?

Darrel never be another you.

Knock, knock.

Who's there?

Les.

Les who?

Les hear some more jokes!

Knock, knock.

Who's there?

Summer.

Summer who?

Summer funny jokes
and summer not.

KNOCK, KNOCK.

WHO'S THERE?

GORILLA.

GORILLA WHO?

GORILLA CHEESE SANDWICH
FOR ME PLEASE.

Knock, knock.

Who's there?

Broken pencil.

Broken pencil who?

Who cares. It's a pointless joke.

Knock, knock.

Who's there?

Watson.

Watson who?

Watson TV tonight?

Knock, knock.

Who's there?

General Lee.

General Lee who?

General Lee I do not tell jokes.

Knock, knock.

Who's there?

Colleen.

Colleen who?

Colleen up your room. It's a mess!

Knock, knock.

Who's there?

Thumping.

Thumping who?

Thumping creepy is crawling up my leg!

Knock, knock.

Who's there?

Isabelle.

Isabelle who?

Isabelle out of order?
I had to knock.

Knock, knock.

Who's there?

Boo.

Boo who?

Why are you crying?

Knock, knock.

Who's there?

Snow.

Snow who?

Snowbody here but me!

Knock, knock.

Who's there?

Wayne.

Wayne who?

Wayne, Wayne, go away.
Come again another day.

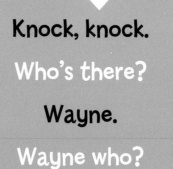

Knock, knock.

Who's there?

Butter.

Butter who?

Butter bring an umbrella.
It looks like rain.

Knock, knock.

Who's there?

Sarah.

Sarah who?

Sarah piece of pizza left?

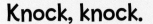

Knock, knock.

Who's there?

Oswald.

Oswald who?

Oswald my gum!

47

Knock, knock.

Who's there?

Justin.

Justin who?

Justin the neighborhood,
and thought I'd drop by.

Knock, knock.

Who's there?

Alma.

Alma who?

Alma candy's gone.

Knock, knock.

Who's there?

A herd.

A herd who?

A herd you were home,
so I came over.

49

Knock, knock.

Who's there?

Shirley.

Shirley who?

Shirley you know more good jokes!

Knock, knock.

Who's there?

Juana.

Juana who?

Juana see a movie tonight?

Knock, knock.

Who's there?

Ben.

Ben who?

Ben looking all over for you.

Knock, knock.

Who's there?

Zombies.

Zombies who?

Zombies make honey,
and zombies don't.

Knock, knock.

Who's there?

Beehive.

Beehive who?

Beehive yourself, or you'll get hurt!

Knock, knock.

Who's there?

Omar.

Omar who?

Omar goodness, wrong door! Sorry!

Knock, knock.

Who's there?

Ach.

Ach who?

Bless you!

Knock, knock.

Who's there?

Anita.

Anita who?

Anita one more minute to get ready.

KNOCK, KNOCK.
WHO'S THERE?
TANK.
TANK WHO?
YOU'RE WELCOME.

Knock, knock.

Who's there?

Hugo.

Hugo who?

Hugo jump in the lake.

Knock, knock.

Who's there?

Luke.

Luke who?

Luke before you leap.

Knock, knock.

Who's there?

Andrew.

Andrew who?

Andrew on the wall, and she is in trouble!

Knock, knock.

Who's there?

Ears.

Ears who?

Ears looking at you, kid.

Knock, knock.

Who's there?

Cash.

Cash who?

Cash me if you can.

KNOCK, KNOCK.
WHO'S THERE?
KANGA.
KANGA WHO?
NO. KANGAROO!

Knock, knock.

Who's there?

Tuna.

Tuna who?

Tuna your radio down.
I can't get to sleep!

Knock, knock.

Who's there?

Amanda.

Amanda who?

Amanda fix the refrigerator.

Knock, knock.

Who's there?

Wood.

Wood who?

Wood you like to go to a movie?

Knock, knock.

Who's there?

Arthur.

Arthur who?

Arthur any cookies left?

KNOCK, KNOCK.
WHO'S THERE?
LETTUCE.
LETTUCE WHO?
LETTUCE IN.
IT'S HOT OUT HERE!

Knock, knock.

Who's there?

Major.

Major who?

Major open the door, didn't I?

Knock, knock.

Who's there?

Needle.

Needle who?

Needle little help?

Knock, knock.

Who's there?

Sherwood.

Sherwood who?

Sherwood like to come inside.

Knock, knock.

Who's there?

Pasta.

Pasta who?

Pasta salt please.

Knock, knock.

Who's there?

Pudding.

Pudding who?

Pudding on your shoes before your socks is a bad idea.

Knock, knock.

Who's there?

Gopher.

Gopher who?

Gopher help. I'm stuck in the mud!

Knock, knock.

Who's there?

Ash.

Ash who?

Ash sure could use some help painting the house.

Knock, knock.

Who's there?

Who.

Who who?

Do you have an owl in there?

Knock, knock.

Who's there?

Stan.

Stan who?

Stan back. I think I'm going to sneeze!

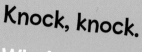

Knock, knock.

Who's there?

Waiter.

Waiter who?

Waiter minute while
I tie my shoes!

69

Knock, knock.

Who's there?

Marsha.

Marsha who?

Marshamallow.

Knock, knock.

Who's there?

Orange juice.

Orange juice who?

Orange juice going to let me in?

Knock, knock.

Who's there?

Gus.

Gus who?

Gus who's coming
to dinner?

Knock, knock.

Who's there?

Sultan.

Sultan who?

Sultan Pepper.

Knock, knock.

Who's there?

Olive.

Olive who?

Olive right next door to you.

Knock, knock.

Who's there?

Stopwatch.

Stopwatch who?

Stopwatch you're doing and let me in!

Knock, knock.

Who's there?

Zookeeper.

Zookeeper who?

Zookeeper away from me!

Knock, knock.

Who's there?

Lena.

Lena who?

Lena little closer, and I'll tell you.

Knock, knock.

Who's there?

Alaska.

Alaska who?

Alaska my mom if you can come over.

Knock, knock.

Who's there?

Lenny.

Lenny who?

Lenny give you a kiss.

Knock, knock.

Who's there?

Duck.

Duck who?

Duck! The neighbors are throwing snowballs!

Knock, knock.

Who's there?

Noah.

Noah who?

Noah good place to play ball?

Knock, knock.

Who's there?

Police.

Police who?

Police open up. It's cold out here!

Knock, knock.

Who's there?

Cotton.

Cotton who?

Cotton in a trap. Please help me!

HOW TO BE FUNNY

KNOCK, KNOCK!

The following tips will help you become rich, famous, and popular. Well, maybe not. However, they will help you tell a good joke.

WHAT TO DO:

- Know the joke.
- Allow suspense to build, but don't drag it out too long.
- Make the punch line clear.
- Be confident, use emotion, and smile.

WHAT NOT TO DO:

- Do not ask your friend over and over if they "get it."
- Do not speak in a different language than your audience.
- Do not tell the same joke every day.
- Do not keep saying, "This joke is so funny!"